Usborne
10 Ten-Minute
Stories

Usborne
10 Ten-Minute Stories

Designed by Laura Nelson
and Lenka Hrehova

CONTENTS

THE KING'S PUDDING

In the middle of the rainforest, the morning sun shone through curtains of lush green leaves. Birds sang, frogs croaked and gibbons whooped and screeched between the trees.

Little Mouse Deer stepped cautiously down to the river to drink. The rainforest was a dangerous place, what with crocodiles in the water and scorpions and snakes in the undergrowth...

...not to mention the mighty, mean tiger, who could snap him up in two quick mouthfuls.

You had to have sharp wits to survive in the forest. How lucky for Mouse Deer that he did – and Tiger didn't.

Looking up from the water,
Mouse Deer saw a flicker of
tawny fur, striped with black,
just like the body of a...
"Tiger!" he gasped.
"Breakfast!" snarled Tiger,
claws unsheathed and
ready to pounce.

Mouse Deer looked around in a panic. "Oh no, I can't possibly be your breakfast," he gabbled. "I have a really important job to do. I'm guarding the King's pudding."

"The King's pudding?" Tiger was puzzled.

Mouse Deer pointed at a brownish cake on the ground. "It's the finest pudding in all the land. It's so delicious that the only person who's allowed to taste it is the King. I have to make sure no one else comes near it."

Tiger looked disappointed. "Couldn't I try just a tiny bite? The King would never know."

"Not a chance," said Mouse Deer. "Unless...
I know! We could pretend you chased me away."

"Brilliant!" said Tiger. "R-ROAR! Off you go then."

Mouse Deer raced through the trees. Closing
his eyes, Tiger took a long lick at the brown cake.

"Bleargh!" His mouth filled with thick river mud. Tiger could taste sludgy earth between his teeth. "MOUSE DEER!" he yelled. "Wait till I catch you!"

Mouse Deer heard Tiger's roars of rage, but he was far away. Surely Tiger would never catch up with him. Settling into the shade of a mighty mangrove tree, Mouse Deer let himself relax.

By midday, the air was heavy and clammy.
Soon the day's rains would start. Insects
chirruped and buzzed, and Mouse
Deer was at the river's edge,
leaning down to drink.

Beyond the bushes, almost out of sight,
were two heavy paws covered in thick,
tawny fur. Almost like the paws of a...
"Tiger!" gasped Mouse Deer.

"Lunch!" growled Tiger, leaping out.
"Oh, I've been looking forward to this!"
Mouse Deer looked around frantically.
"I can't possibly be your lunch," he protested.
"Not while I'm guarding the King's belt."

"The King's belt?" Tiger was suspicious.

"There, do you see, on that branch? Isn't it magnificent?" Mouse Deer pointed to a jewel-bright loop. "Of course, no one else is allowed to wear it. Such a pity. It would really suit you."

"But the King would never know," whined Tiger. "How could he guess you'd let me try his belt?"

"Someone else might tell him," said Mouse Deer darkly. "Unless... unless they saw you chasing me away, of course."

Tiger opened his mouth to roar, but Mouse Deer was already gone. Tiger shrugged, and reached up to pull the belt down from the branch.

He wrapped it around his waist, once, twice... ...and it began to writhe. Then it hissed in fury. Tiger's beautiful belt was a snake! Maddened, the snake sank its fangs into Tiger's soft, furry belly.

"YOWWWW!!"

Far upstream, Mouse Deer paused when he heard Tiger's roar of pain. Then he ran on a little further, just to be on the safe side.

By the evening, the rains had stopped and the
new moon rose into a clear sky. Fireflies gleamed
in the shadows, and Mouse Deer pattered down to
the river's edge for a drink.

Two fierce eyes were watching him steadily,
just like the eyes of a...

"Tiger!" gasped Mouse Deer.

"Dinner!" roared Tiger. "And don't think you can talk me out of eating you this time!"

Mouse Deer looked around desperately. There was a faint buzzing in his ears. "No, no, no," he cried. "You can't! Not while I'm guarding the King's drum!"

"The King's drum?" snorted Tiger.

"Look above you." A dark shape hung from the tree. "Such a drum! It may not be much to look at, but the sound! It's like magic. People say when you hear it, you just can't help dancing."

"And I suppose only the King is allowed to play it," said Tiger huffily.

"Oh yes! Not that the King is a very good drummer. You'd be much better, I can tell. You have a natural rhythm."

"It's not fair!" Tiger grumbled. "Why should the King have a drum he can't even play? Why can't anyone else play it? Let me try. You can say you didn't see me until it was too late. Or... I know! You can say I scared you away!"

"Far, far away," agreed Mouse Deer, taking to his heels.

Tiger puffed up his chest, and reached for the drum. To his surprise, it broke away from the branch where it was hanging and fell at his feet.

A swarm of angry wasps poured out, stinging poor Tiger again and again, until at last he dived into the cool green river.

"Mouse Deer!" Tiger roared. "Mouse Deer, I give up! I have a mouth full of mud, a snake-bitten belly and my paws are covered in wasp stings! AND I STILL HAVEN'T HAD MY DINNER!

Oh, you're too clever for me, Mouse Deer! I promise I'll never try to catch you again!"

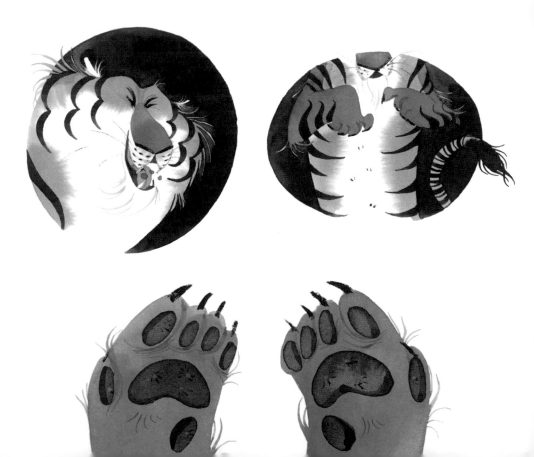

Mouse Deer hadn't had time to run very far after all. Hidden behind a bush, he heard Tiger's roar, and smiled to himself. He had survived one more day in the forest.

THE
TIN SOLDIER

om leaped out of bed and tugged on his clothes. Today his grandpa was coming to stay for a week. Grandpa was full of fun ideas and he always brought Tom a wonderful present.

"Here you are, Tom!" said Grandpa, handing him a large box.

"Wow, tin soldiers!" Tom cried. "Thank you," he added, as he lifted the lid.

"Oh dear!" said Grandpa, taking out a soldier. "This fellow only has one leg."

Tom didn't mind.

Attention!

He spent all day marching his new toys around the playroom and up and down the stairs.

At bedtime, Tom reluctantly packed his soldiers back in their box. As he put them in, he realized one was missing.

"Hey, where's my one-legged soldier?" Tom wondered. "He was the one I liked best."

He hunted everywhere, but the seventh tin soldier was nowhere to be found.

"Never mind, Tom," said Grandpa. "You can look for him in the morning."

Tom climbed into bed with a sigh and snuggled down under the bedclothes. After the day's marching, he was soon fast asleep.

"Yipee!" came a tiny cry from beneath his bed. "Now it's our turn to have some fun."

Soon, robots and building blocks were racing across the floor of the playroom. A flying saucer whizzed around in circles, with a pirate captain clinging on for all he was worth.

"Ha har, me hearty!" chuckled the pirate to the space pilot. "If only Tom could see us now."

Woo hoo!

The six tin soldiers were desperate
to join in the fun.

But no matter how hard they pushed
and squeezed, they couldn't break free
of their box. The one-legged soldier was
luckier. He scrambled out from beneath
a pile of plastic blocks and looked
around the room.

Opposite him stood a fairy palace
that belonged to Tom's sister, and
in the doorway was a dancer
made of paper.

"She's beautiful," thought the soldier, as the ballerina spun and twirled on one leg, "and so graceful. She would be the perfect wife for me."

The paper ballerina noticed the soldier peeking out from the blocks and blushed. The more she danced, the more the tin soldier fell helplessly in love. The ballerina smiled. No one had ever admired her dancing as much as this handsome soldier.

One of the other toys had noticed the soldier and the ballerina staring at each other – and he was not happy.

A sudden BOING! made the soldier jump.

"Keep your eyes off that ballerina!"
snapped a bad-tempered jack-in-the-box.
"I'm going to marry her. So stay away!"

But the tin soldier wouldn't be put off so easily. Ignoring the fuming jack-in-the-box, he hopped over to the palace. He plucked one of the flowers that covered the walls and nervously offered it to the ballerina.

"Your dancing was the most beautiful thing I've ever seen," said the soldier.

"Why thank you," replied the ballerina.

The jack-in-the-box growled. "I've warned you once, soldier," he said, through gritted teeth. "If you don't back off, there's going to be trouble."

The brave soldier didn't care. He and the ballerina chatted and chuckled together until dawn.

The next morning, Tom awoke to find the one-legged soldier on the palace steps.

"How did you get there?" said Tom, placing his toy on the windowsill.

"Look out, soldier!" cried the other toys as loudly as they dared.

The jack-in-the-box was staring wickedly at his rival. The other toys knew that stare: it meant danger. The soldier glanced behind him... Too late.

The jack-in-the-box took a huge breath and blew the soldier off his foot. The poor toy wobbled and tottered, before tumbling head first out of the open window.

"Ha, ha!" cackled the jack-in-the-box. "That's the last we'll see of him."

The tin soldier landed with a clang
on the street outside.

"Ouch!" he moaned.

Just then, he heard pounding footsteps
and two boys rushed up, grinning.

"Look, Harry!" yelled one. "A tin soldier."

"You're right, Joe. Hey, let's turn him into a sailor," laughed Harry. He grabbed an old newspaper that was blowing along the street. With a few folds, he transformed it into a boat.

Joe popped the soldier into the boat and Harry lowered it into a puddle by the side of the road.

One push and the boat sailed away, carrying the trembling tin soldier.

"I feel sea sick," thought the soldier, clutching his tummy as the boat twisted and swirled.

As he sailed on, he began to wonder if he'd ever see the ballerina and the other toys again. Then the paper boat picked up speed and the soldier found himself hurtling towards a dark drain hole.

"Aaaagh!"

The boat plunged over the edge and fell SPLAT! into the smelly, sludgy sewer below.

"Pew!" spat the soldier, holding his nose.

The boat sailed on into the darkness.

Moments later, a dirty rat scuttled out from the shadows. "Pay me a penny to pass!" he demanded.

"Sorry!" called the soldier, as his little craft spun past. "I'm afraid I don't have any money."

Must dash, Rat!

Come back here!

Just when he thought he would never see daylight again, the soldier shot out of the drain and landed SPLOSH! in a river.

By now the paper boat was so soggy it sank.

"Glug, glug, glug..." said the soldier as he dropped below the surface.

Down and down he fell. He had almost reached the riverbed when a huge fish swam up.

"Ah, lunch!" thought the fish with a greedy grin. He opened his mouth and gobbled down the soldier. "Tinny," thought the fish, "but not bad."

"It looks as if I'll be stuck in this fish forever," sighed the soldier. He shut his eyes and dreamed of the lovely ballerina.

Little did the soldier know, but his luck was about to change.

An angler by the river hooked the fish on his line. "What a whopper!" gasped the man. "I'll get a great price for this beauty." He rushed into town with his catch and laid it out proudly on his market stall.

Who should buy it, but Tom's grandpa? He took the fish home, unwrapped it and the tin soldier slipped out of the fish's mouth and clanked onto the kitchen table.

Grandpa could hardly believe his eyes. "Tom! Tom!" he called, rushing to show him. Tom had been so sad since his new toy had gone missing.

"Look who I found!" said Grandpa with a smile.

"My one-legged soldier!" cried Tom.

Tom spent the rest of the day playing with the tin soldier.

That night, the delighted toys gathered
around to welcome back their friend.
Everyone was pleased to see him.
Well, nearly everyone...

I'm so glad
you're home!

Yipee!

Phooey!

The jack-in-the-box was so cross, he bounced up and down for an hour.

Eventually his springs couldn't take any more. PING! went one. DOING! went another.

With a last gasp, he flopped over and never worked again.

A few days later, the tin soldier and
the paper ballerina were married.
All the toys were invited
to the wedding.

"Hooray for the happy couple!" they shouted.

There was singing and dancing until dawn –
and Tom never knew a thing about it.

BEAUTY AND THE BEAST

Once, there was a gentle girl named Beauty, who lived with her two sisters and their father, Felix, a rich merchant. All three girls loved their father. Beauty's sisters loved his money too.

One day, Felix was heading to market. "What presents shall I bring back?" he asked.

"Ooh, lots of jewels and silken dresses," said Beauty's sisters.

"May I have a rose?" asked Beauty.

Felix smiled. "Is that all? Of course!"

Felix had a successful trip and set off home with his bags full of presents for Beauty's sisters. But he hadn't found a single rose. He was still worrying about it when a thick mist swirled around him. In minutes, he was completely and utterly lost.

At last the mist cleared, and he saw a castle ahead. "I'll ask for directions there," he thought.

As he rode closer and the castle loomed above him, Felix began to feel afraid. "Who would live in such a lonely spot?" he wondered.

He went to knock on the front door. Silently, it swung open.

"Hello?" he called. "Is anyone here?"

No one answered. The only sound was his own voice, echoing around the stone walls.

"What *is* this place?" murmured Felix.

A mouthwatering smell drifted down the corridor, tempting him further in... until he reached a grand banqueting hall. A long table was laid with a sumptuous feast, and candles flickered in welcome.

"Where is everyone?" he thought.

As if in a trance, he walked over to the table
and sat down, only to gasp with astonishment
when a full plate of food floated over to him.
Invisible hands filled a goblet with ruby-red wine.
Nervously, Felix picked up a knife and fork.

He felt a little uncomfortable helping himself
but there was no one to ask and he was starving.

"Besides," he decided, "the castle seems to want
me to eat."

After the meal, he wandered outside, hoping to find someone in the garden.

To his delight, what he found was a rosebush blooming with sweet-scented buds.

"Beauty's rose!" he thought. "I'm sure nobody will mind if I just pick one..."

"HOW DARE YOU?" roared a voice.

A monstrous beast leaped from the shadows and pointed a sword at Felix's throat.

"I give you food and you repay me by STEALING?" snarled the Beast.

"I didn't mean to steal," Felix said, shaking all over. "It was for my daughter, Beauty."

"Send her to me," said the Beast, "and you may live. If she refuses, you must return at dawn."

"*I* will be the one to return," Felix declared. "Just, *please* let me see my daughters one last time."

The Beast gave him an enchanted red bridle to guide him home. With a heavy heart, Felix put it on his horse and rode away.

"Father!" cried Beauty, rushing out to greet him when he arrived home. "How was the market?"

"That was fine," said her father, with a brave smile. "But, oh my dearest Beauty, something dreadful happened. I upset a grotesque beast and have promised to return to his castle at dawn."

"What? How? Why?" Beauty began, but her father refused to say more.

"It doesn't matter," he insisted. "Let me spend one last happy evening with my family."

Beauty couldn't bear the thought of her father becoming the slave of some hideous creature. "I have to ask him to spare Father," she decided.

The next morning, she got up well before dawn and saddled her father's horse. A bright red bridle hung on a peg nearby so she put that on too.

She thought she would head to the market first, but she was barely in the saddle before the horse galloped off, flying along unfamiliar paths. As they left a shadowy forest, a castle came into view.

Beauty paused at the steps leading to the castle. The thought of meeting the Beast terrified her, but then she remembered her father.

Taking a deep breath, she dropped the horse's reins and began to climb.

A hideous figure stood in the hall.

Was this the Beast?

He looked so sad, Beauty forgot her fear.

"What is it? What's wrong?" she asked.

"I'm lonely," he sniffed, wiping away a tear.
"But who are you?"

"Beauty," said Beauty.
"I came to ask you to
save my father."

Beauty's courage impressed the Beast. "Your father is spared," he said. "But, I wonder, would you share a meal with me before you go home?"

Beauty nodded and sat down to the most delicious breakfast she had ever eaten. The Beast told funny stories and Beauty told him all about her family.

After breakfast, the Beast knelt down before Beauty and cleared his throat nervously. "This may seem sudden," he said, "and I know I am an ugly creature, but... will you marry me?"

Beauty gasped. "Marry you?" she said. "I barely know you! But I will keep you company here for a week, if you let my father know I am safe."

The Beast told Beauty she could go where she wished, and she explored every room in the castle. The one she liked best was the library. Its shelves seemed to reach the sky, filled with magical books.

The Beast looked after her wonderfully. She grew so fond of him, she even forgot how he looked.

Each evening after dinner, the Beast knelt before her.

"Dear, sweet Beauty, will you marry me?"

"Oh Beast," Beauty sighed. "I like you so much, but I don't love you. I cannot marry you."

Every night, the Beast asked his question and, every night, Beauty refused.

On the seventh evening, he produced a ring.

"Oh Beast, I'm sorry, I really am, but I won't marry you!" Beauty cried.

"This isn't an engagement ring," said the Beast, sadly. "It's a magic ring to take you home." And he placed it on her finger.

A fizzing
feeling spread
through Beauty's
body and she
found herself
whirling through
the air.

She landed with a jolt
back home. There was her
father, waiting to welcome
her, with open arms and a
beaming smile.

"Beauty!" he shouted,
sweeping her into a hug.

Beauty was thrilled to be home but she couldn't help missing the Beast. Then, one night, she woke with a start. In her dream, the Beast lay dying, calling out her name.

Beauty threw on a dress and grasped the magic ring. "Take me to the castle," she begged.

A familiar fizzing spread through her and she whirled through the air, to land in the corridor that led to the garden.

For a second, she stood, catching her breath.

Then she picked up her skirts and ran.

The Beast was sprawled on the ground,
just as she'd pictured him in her dream.

"Beast?" she cried.

The Beast struggled to open his eyes. "Beauty?"
he said weakly. "Is that you?"

"Yes, I'm here," she reassured him, "but what's wrong? Why are you so ill?"

"I'm dying," the Beast whispered.

"No!" Beauty was horrified. She stroked his velvety face. "You can't die. Please Beast. I–I love you," she blurted out, realizing suddenly that it was true.

A roaring wind blasted Beauty back, as a blinding flash forced her to close her eyes. When she opened them again, a handsome prince was kneeling beside her.

"Who are you? Where's my Beast?" she asked.

"I'm the Beast," the Prince smiled. "Many years ago, a wicked fairy cursed me when I refused to marry her. Only the love of a beautiful girl could save me. She said if I loved someone who didn't love me, I would die of a broken heart."

"But I do love you," Beauty cried joyously. "And if you ask me once more to marry you, the answer will be yes!"

WHY THE
SEA IS SALTY

Long ago, they say, the sea wasn't salty as it is today. Once, it was as pure and sweet as springwater – so pure that sailors could scoop it up and drink it whenever they felt thirsty. So where did the salt come from?

The story begins with
a magic millstone...

This millstone belonged to a great king. The king owned many precious things, but there was nothing he prized more than the millstone.

Most millstones are used for making flour. But this one was different. For a start, it turned by itself.

And when it turned, it didn't make flour. Sometimes, it made glittering heaps of gold and jewels.

Sometimes, it made sackfuls of rare herbs and exotic spices. In fact, it made whatever the king wished for.

84

So the king's treasure chests were always full. His food was always delicious. And it was all thanks to his amazing magic millstone.

One day, a thief was sipping tea when he heard about the millstone. "I'll steal it," he thought. "It'll make me rich! I just need to find out where it's kept..."

The thief put on his best clothes and went to
the palace. He told the guards he had come from
a long way away, just to see where the king lived.
"I've heard the palace is magnificent," he said.

WHY THE SEA IS SALTY

A kind guard offered to show him around.
First, they walked through the gardens.
There were beautiful flowers and peaceful
ponds... but no sign of a millstone.

Then they visited the throne room. There were towering columns and a high red throne... but no sign of a millstone.

Last of all, they came to the royal bed chamber. The thief still couldn't see a millstone, but a mattress on the floor made him wonder...

"I'm sorry not to see the famous magic millstone," he sighed. "I suppose it's kept hidden away?"

"Of course," said the guard, with a laugh. "It's much too valuable to leave lying around."

"I bet I can guess where it's hidden," said the thief. "Up a chimney?"

"Don't be silly," said the guard. "That would be too smoky!"

"Under the floorboards?" went on the thief.

"No, no," said the guard. "Too dusty!"

"I don't believe you even know where it's kept," teased the thief.

"Oh yes I do," said the guard proudly.

"It's under the king's bed!"

"And I suppose you have to be a great magician to work the millstone?" the thief went on.

"Oh no," said the guard. "I've seen the king. You just tap it three times and say what you want."

The thief left the palace with a cheery wave.

"Thanks for the tour," he told the guard. "You were a big help." He grinned as he walked away. "More help than you know," he added, under his breath.

Later that day, the thief sneaked back again. Silently, he scaled a wall and slunk through the grounds towards the palace.

Once inside, he tiptoed to the empty bed chamber, reached under the mattress... and felt something hard and round and made of stone.

"Got it!" he thought triumphantly.

He pulled the millstone out and gazed at it
briefly in delight. Then, he hid it under his cloak
and ran away as fast as he could.

He ran all the way to the sea. A boat bobbed by
the water's edge. It didn't belong to him, but he
didn't care. He leaped in and sailed away.

Once he was safely at sea, he pulled out the millstone. "What shall I ask for first?" he mused. While he was thinking, he unwrapped a bun and took a big bite.

"Pah!" he spat in disgust. "That needs salt."
Then he grinned. "I know what to ask for."

He tapped the millstone three times and said
loudly: "I want salt."

At once, the millstone began to turn – and a
sparkling stream of bright, white salt poured out.

"I did it!" cried the thief, whooping in delight.

He sprinkled some salt on his bun and munched away happily. Then he fell asleep under the stars, dreaming of the riches that would soon be his.

Meanwhile, the millstone
kept turning. The pile of salt
grew bigger...

...and bigger. The
thief snored happily,
completely unaware.

By morning, the pile was
ENORMOUS. As the boat
rocked, some of the salt
trickled down and tickled
the thief's feet.
    Finally, he
opened his
eyes...

There, before him, was a brilliant white
mountain of salt. "Stupid stone," he snapped.
"Stop!" But the millstone kept turning... and the
mountain kept growing.

"Didn't you hear?" he yelled crossly. "I said STOP!"

But the millstone kept turning... and the mountain kept growing.

As the mountain grew larger and larger,
the boat sank lower and lower in the water.
Before long, waves were slopping over
the sides...

...and still the
millstone kept turning.
"I'll throw it overboard,"
thought the thief. He dug
desperately through the salt,
searching. But the millstone
was buried too deep.

With a glug and a gurgle, the boat sank, taking the magic millstone with it to the bottom of the ocean. There it has stayed, pouring out salt to this very day. And that, so they say, is why the sea is salty.

As for the thief, he had to swim all the way
home, and when he finally splashed ashore, there
was an angry king waiting for him. So he never did
get his riches – only a spell in jail with wet clothes
and a bad cold. *Aaaa-choo!*

THE STORY OF PEGASUS

The king of Lycia had a problem – in the shape of a youth named Bellerophon. The king's allies wanted him to kill the boy, who was staying in the palace. "What am I going to do?" mused the king. "I *can't* kill a guest..." Then he smiled.

"But I *can* send him on a doomed quest."

The king spoke to Bellerophon that night. "There's a terrible monster ravaging my lands," he said. "It's named the Chimera. I need you to kill it."

Bellerophon gulped. He couldn't refuse the king, but he had heard stories of the Chimera... "I'll, um, leave tomorrow," he said, trying to sound brave.

The Chimera, people said, had the head of a
lion, the body of a goat and a snake for a tail. It
spat venom and breathed fire. Many men had tried
to kill it – and all of them had failed.

"How on earth can I kill such a beast?" muttered
Bellerophon, as he left the palace.

"You will need the help of the gods," answered a voice. Bellerophon jumped. A wizened old man had appeared beside him.

"Do you see the temple on the hill?" the man asked. "Sleep there tonight and help will come."

As the stars shone down, Bellerophon
dreamed... A goddess stood before him,
holding out a golden bridle.

"Go to the mountains," she said, "and
wait for Pegasus, the winged horse. You
can tame him with this bridle."

"With Pegasus, you will be able to fight the Chimera from the air. Now sleep..."

When Bellerophon woke, a golden bridle glittered in his hands.

"So it wasn't just a dream," he gasped, "and Pegasus can be mine!" He set off for the mountains at once.

Bellerophon found Pegasus drinking from a mountain stream. The horse's coat and wings gleamed pearly white, and his hooves flashed gold in the morning sun. Bellerophon sighed in admiration. Quietly, he crept closer...

Pegasus reared up, beating the air with his
powerful wings. Quick as a flash, Bellerophon
slipped the bridle over Pegasus' head –
and at once, the horse grew calm.

"Let's go," cried Bellerophon, swinging himself up onto Pegasus' back. "Take to the skies!"

Obediently, the horse leaped into the air. They soared higher and higher, over treetops and mountains, up into the airy blue.

In the distance Bellerophon spied a puff of smoke. "The Chimera!" he thought, turning towards it...

The Chimera had made its lair
in a rocky wilderness. Pegasus
hovered high above on beating
wings as the monster belched
smoke and fire. Even from the
sky, Bellerophon could feel the
scorching heat.

"Time to attack," he decided, urging his horse lower. He raised his bow and arrow, took careful aim and fired. The Chimera roared with fury and shot out a huge blast of flames.

Bellerophon pulled
Pegasus out of the way
just in time.

They spun around and swooped back. As the
Chimera opened its mouth to shoot out more fire,
Bellerophon leaned over and plunged his spear
deep into the monster's throat.

The spearhead melted in the monster's fiery
breath. The Chimera struggled, rose up in one
last effort... then slumped to the ground, dead.
Bellerophon had won.

The king was amazed when Bellerophon returned in triumph. "You are a hero," he told Bellerophon. And, for a while, he was. Everywhere he went, he was greeted by cheering crowds.

Soon, Bellerophon began to think he was better
than everyone else. "I belong with the gods,"
he declared. "Not with ordinary men."

He swung himself onto Pegasus and flew up
through the clouds, up to the highest mountain
of all: Mount Olympus, the home of the gods.

Bellerophon's arrogance infuriated Zeus, the
king of the gods. "How dare you come here?"
he thundered. "No mortal can live with the gods.
Without Pegasus, you are nothing."

Zeus sent an insect to sting Pegasus, making the horse buck and rear. Bellerophon fell, tumbling down through the blue sky...

...and crashing back to Earth in a dazed, miserable heap. Now, no one would go near him, because he had angered the gods. He was left to wander alone for the rest of his days.

But Pegasus had a different fate. "Unlike your upstart master, you *do* belong on Olympus," Zeus told the horse. Gently, he took hold of the golden bridle and led the magical horse home.

From that day on, Pegasus lived with the gods, pulling Zeus in his chariot. As a reward for his faithful service, when Pegasus eventually died, Zeus placed him among the stars.

If you look up at the night sky, you might see him there today.

DICK WHITTINGTON

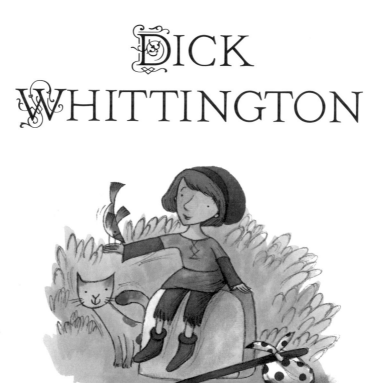

There once was a boy named Dick Whittington.
He didn't have a home, or a mother and
father to look after him. His only friends were the
animals he met as he wandered the countryside.

When Dick was hungry, he had to hunt
for berries on prickly bushes, or scramble
up tall trees for apples or pears.

Wooah!

But that wasn't his only problem...

He spent so long
roaming the rough country
roads, the soles of his
boots were worn
right through.

Every time he
stepped on a sharp
stone, he winced.

My poor
feet!

"I can't go on like
this," thought Dick one
cold, wet day, as he sat
shivering beneath an
oak tree. "I need
some money, and that
means finding a job.
I'll start looking first
thing tomorrow."

The next morning, he met a boatman.

"Excuse me, sir," cried Dick. "I'm looking for work. Can I help you ferry people across the river?"

"Sorry, son," called the boatman. "This is a one-man job."

Dick spoke to builders and blacksmiths. But the reply was always the same.

Sorry, son. No work here.

Dick was determined not to give up. So when he saw a farmer working away in his field, Dick rushed up eagerly.

"I'm after a job," he panted. "I could milk your cows, or make hay, or plant vegetables, or..."

"Woah there, sonny!" said the farmer. He sighed. "I'd love to find you work, but I'm a poor man myself."

"Oh well, thanks anyway," sniffed Dick sadly.

"You should try London," said the farmer. "They say the streets there are paved with gold."

Gold?

That's right.

His heart racing, Dick thanked the farmer and
strode off along the road to London.

His head was full of ideas for how he would
spend the riches that awaited him.

"I could buy a whole crate of apples," he thought,
licking his lips, "or a hundred crates, maybe!"

He looked down at his feet. "What's more, I'll
get myself the finest, toughest boots that money
can buy."

Dick was so excited that the first few miles whizzed by without him even noticing.

But as the day wore on, he began to realize just how far he had to travel. By the time the sun was setting, he'd slowed down to a snail's pace.

"I must... keep... going," he panted wearily.

LONDON
14 MILES

At dawn, Dick arrived on the outskirts of the city.
He was soon caught up in the hustle and bustle of
market traders getting ready for business.

But his excitement quickly turned to
disappointment. The streets weren't paved with
gold at all, just dirty old stone.

Once again,
Dick set about
looking for
work. He asked
a busy baker...

...a butcher carrying some ducks
to sell at his stall in the market...

...and a cobbler tapping
away at a pair of boots.
But everywhere it was
the same story. No one
could give him a job.

By now, it was
getting dark. The
traders began
heading for home, and
the streets became deserted.
Dick was tired out after a long day
trudging through the city. He flopped down on
the steps of a grand house and yawned. Barely able
to keep his eyes open, he quickly dozed off.

"Get off my steps!" shouted a harsh voice.

It was the next morning and Dick woke to see
an angry woman waving
a rolling pin at him.

Get out of here!

Dick rubbed his eyes and
scrambled to his feet. He was about
to run off when a richly-dressed man appeared
in the doorway.

"I found this scallywag asleep on the steps,
Mr. Fitzwarren," barked the woman.

The man looked at Dick. "I expect the poor boy
needs a decent meal," he said. "Bring him inside,
Mrs. Grump."

While Mrs. Grump waddled off to make breakfast, Mr. Fitzwarren showed Dick around.

Dick had never been in such an incredible house. It was filled with strange and wonderful things.

"I'm a sea trader," explained Mr. Fitzwarren. "My ships bring back goods from all over the world."

Over breakfast, Dick told Mr. Fitzwarren his story. The kind man decided to give Dick a job helping out in his kitchen. Dick couldn't believe his luck.

He started by peeling a mountain of carrots.

It was hard work, but Dick didn't mind. The only bad part was being bossed by Mrs. Grump, who spent the whole day shouting and moaning at him.

"I don't know why the master let you into this house," she grumbled.

Out of my way!

That evening, Mr. Fitzwarren showed Dick up to a room in the attic.

Dick had never slept in such comfort.

He snuggled down under the blanket and drifted off to sleep. It didn't last long.

"Scratch, scratch!" came a noise from beneath his bed. Dick woke to see four fat mice scrabbling on the floorboards.

They were joined by four more. Soon the whole room was filled with mice scurrying across Dick's bed, scampering over his pillow and climbing in and out of his boots.

How can I sleep now?

Dick hardly got a wink of sleep. It happened the next night and the night after that. Poor Dick stumbled around exhausted and bleary-eyed.

On Friday morning, Mr. Fitzwarren handed Dick his first week's wages.

A whole penny! Thanks.

Dick had never had any money of his own. He couldn't wait to spend it at the nearby market.

There were so many
stalls in the marketplace,
Dick couldn't decide
where to begin. There
were people selling fruit
and vegetables, clothes
and brightly patterned
cloth. Then a purring
caught Dick's attention.

Kittens
1 penny

Frog starter kit
1 penny

Puppies
2 pennies

He rushed over to the pet stall
and scooped up a soft furry kitten.
"You're just what I need
to deal with those noisy mice,"
he whispered.

He handed over his penny to
the stallkeeper and carried home his
new pet. "I'll call you Tom," he said.

When Dick went to bed that night,
the mice sneaked out as usual. But this
time, Dick was ready.

"After them, Tom!" he cried, and the
little cat leaped into action. Mice scattered
in all directions as Tom chased them around
the room and back below the floorboards.

From then on, no mouse dared show his
whiskers in the attic, and Dick slept soundly.

A few days later, Mr. Fitzwarren called his staff into his study. "One of my ships is setting sail on a trading mission," he announced. "If any of you have something to sell, it can go on the ship."

Dick knew that Mr. Fitzwarren had made his fortune by buying and selling things. Perhaps if Dick sold something, he could be rich too? The problem was, he only owned one thing – Tom.

Dick didn't really want to part with his kitten. He'd grown very fond of him.

"But maybe someone would pay me *two* pennies for him," he thought.

Reluctantly, Dick decided to offer Tom for sale. The next morning, he loaded his kitten onto a cart along with the other items bound for Mr. Fitzwarren's ship.

"Bye Tom!" he called sadly as the cart trundled away.

That night, Dick
discovered his mistake.
As soon as the mice
realized Tom was no
longer around, they
crawled out of their
hiding places.

More sleepless nights
followed. Dick was
tired and slow, and Mrs.
Grump started bullying
him again.

Dick decided he had to
go. Early one morning, he
crept from the house.

As Dick walked away from London, he could hear the church bells ringing behind him.

To his surprise, they seemed to be calling out a message:

♪ Turn again Whittington,
thrice mayor of London.

"They're telling me to go back," Dick thought in amazement.

He didn't understand how bells could talk. But it seemed crazy not to follow their advice. He turned on his heels and rushed back to Mr. Fitzwarren's.

When he arrived, Mr. Fitzwarren was waiting on the doorstep.

"Ah, there you are, Dick," he cried with a grin. "Good news! The King of Barbary bought your cat to clear the mice from his palace. He sent you these two bags of gold in payment."

"Gold!" thought Dick. "I am glad I listened to those bells."

Dick saved the money, and when he grew up he became a trader like Mr. Fitzwarren. Not only that, but he also became Mayor of London three times...

Hooray for Mayor Whittington!

...just as the bells had said.

THE

MAGIC GIFTS

Once upon a time, there was a rich merchant named Chung-Hee. He lived in a grand house in Korea with his three sons – Bong, Yong and Chin.

One winter, Chung-Hee became very ill. Fearing the worst, he gathered his sons to his bedside.

"When I'm gone," he croaked, "promise that you'll share my fortune equally between you."

"Of course, Father," replied the three boys.

A few weeks later, Chung-Hee died.

"Now we must divide Father's fortune," declared Bong. "I'm the eldest, so I should have the biggest share."

"I'm the second eldest," cried Yong. "So I should have the second biggest share."

By the time Chin's greedy brothers had taken their share of the money, he was left with just one tiny bag of coins.

Bong and Yong went on a spending spree. They crammed the house from roof to cellar with expensive china and fine furniture.

"Sorry, Chin, there's simply no room here for you any more," Yong announced one day.

"You'll have to find somewhere else to live," agreed Bong. "Bye!"

Chin went into the village. But instead of spending his money on himself, he helped the poor locals.

He bought them food...

...and warm robes to keep out the biting winter winds.

He even paid their rents. Soon all of the coins in his little bag were gone.

Meanwhile, Chin's brothers were still rolling in money.

"What shall we spend our loot on next?" asked Bong, fanning himself with a wad of cash.

"We need a bigger house for a start," said Yong.

The pair moved into a magnificent new home.

"It's fit for an emperor," said Yong.

Bong grinned. "Let's dress like emperors then!"

They had the best tailors make them robes of smooth silk and rich velvet.

"Now we need some sparkle," said Yong.

So they decorated their new clothes with glittering rings and dazzling necklaces.

The pair were showing off their new outfits in the village when they stumbled across Chin, wandering along the road. His clothes were worn and his face was dirty.

"We can't let people see our brother looking so scruffy," whispered Bong.

Yong agreed. "You're making us look bad, Chin," he said. "It's embarrassing. You'll have to leave."

Chin trudged sadly out of the village and into the forest. It was an eerie, creepy place, where the trees were carved with strange faces.

Emerging from the forest, Chin saw a river. He was cooling his feet in the water when an elderly monk appeared.

"Can you help me across?" he panted. "The bridge has broken."

"Okay," said Chin. The old man clambered onto his back and Chin waded across the river.

"Could you carry me home?" asked the monk faintly. "It's a long way for an old man with a heavy load."

Chin felt sorry for the monk. So he took him all the way to his house, high up on a mountain.

When the monk discovered that Chin was penniless, he invited him to stay. In return, Chin helped around the house. He swept the floors...

...mended the monk's clothes when they became worn...

...and copied out the monk's books in big letters, so he could read them more easily.

After Chin had been with the monk for six weeks, the old man decided he should return home. "Please take this reward for your kindness," he said.

And he handed Chin an old straw mat, a wooden spoon and a pair of chopsticks. "You'll find them useful," he added with a grin.

With a wave goodbye, Chin set off. By the time
he reached the forest it was late evening. Feeling
tired, he rolled out the straw mat and lay down.

"I wish I had a nice comfy bed to sleep in,"
he murmured, as he drifted off to sleep.

When he woke up, he got the shock of his life.

He was no longer in the forest. Instead, he
found himself lying on a huge, luxurious bed
in a wonderful palace bursting with treasures.

"My wish came true!" thought Chin. As he climbed out of bed, he saw the straw mat under the mattress. "Maybe the monk's mat was magic? I wonder if the other things were too?"

He tugged the spoon from his pocket. "I wish I had something to eat," he declared. In an instant, a stream of delicious juicy fruit flew from the spoon.

Chin feasted on the fruit in delight. It was the finest meal he had ever eaten.

Then he looked down at his tattered clothes. "Hardly fit for a palace," he thought.

He took out the chopsticks and gave them a click. "I wish I had some fine robes," he cried. There was a whirl of shimmering silk, and Chin's wish came true.

A few days later, Chin's brothers were passing the forest when they saw a fantastic jade palace in the distance.

"I've never noticed that before," said Bong.

"It must belong to people even richer than us," said Yong. "We should introduce ourselves. Who knows where it might lead?"

Bong and Yong couldn't believe their eyes when they met the owner of the palace.

"Chin!" they cried. "How did you become so rich?"

Chin told them about the monk and the three magic gifts.

"Maybe if we were poor, the monk would give us magic gifts too," whispered Yong to Bong.

The brothers rushed
home and gave away
all their money
and jewels...

...every piece of their
fabulous furniture...

...and all their
fine clothes,
until only their
tattered old
robes were left.

Then they ran through the forest, across the river and up the mountain to the monk's house. But the old man wasn't there.

"I expect he'll be back soon," said Yong.

"Yes, it'll be worth the wait," agreed Bong.

And so they waited... and waited... and waited...

The hours turned to days. The days turned to weeks. The weeks turned to a year.

At last, threadbare and starving, the two brothers gave up and staggered back to Chin's palace.

"I don't suppose Chin will take us in after we were so mean to him," sighed Bong, full of shame. But Chin welcomed them back with open arms.

"I forgive you both," Chin said with a smile. "A happy family is the most precious gift of all."

THE

FIREBIRD

There was once a king who had everything in life he could possibly want. He ruled over a vast kingdom, he lived in a magnificent palace and he had three brave sons.

The king was surrounded by beautiful things, but his greatest treasure was a garden.

Its trees blossomed with fine jewels, and in the middle was an apple tree with fruit of solid gold.

One morning, the king was horrified to see that a golden apple was missing from the tree.

"A thief in my garden?" he roared. "How can this be?"

The king's eldest son spoke up. "Father, let me keep watch tonight. I will catch the thief for you." As the night wore on, the prince leaned against the apple tree to rest. His eyes grew heavy...

He woke at dawn. With horror, he saw that another apple had been taken. "How could the thief have reached it without my knowing?"

The next night, his brother took his place, but he, too, drifted into sleep.

"Let me keep watch," said Ivan, the king's youngest son.

"You?" sneered his brothers. "As if you could do anything! You're hardly more than a boy!"

In the starry dark, Ivan walked around the
garden, singing songs. Just before dawn, the sky
grew bright. A beautiful fiery bird swooped down
to the tree, seizing an apple in her long beak.

Ivan leaped up to catch her, but she pulled free.
He was left clutching a single feather from her tail.

The king was astonished to hear Ivan's story, and his brothers could hardly contain their envy.

"What a marvel!" sighed the king. "If I had that bird, I would be the envy of a dozen kingdoms."

"I will find her for you," said his eldest son at once. "Go, saddle my horse and summon my servants. I will set out this instant."

Weeks passed before the prince returned.

"I have searched the whole kingdom," he complained. "There is no trace of her."

"I will go further, and search harder," claimed his brother, but he, too, came home disappointed.

"I don't believe she even exists," he grumbled.

By the time Ivan set out, it was midwinter and snow lay deep on the ground. The icy air scoured his face, but beneath his cloak, the Firebird's feather glowed and kept him warm.

In the stillness of the forest, he seemed to hear ghostly voices. "Go back, go back," they urged, "or the wolves will get you!"

With a savage snarl, a huge silvery wolf sprang
from the trees and attacked his horse. Ivan drew
his sword, but before he could land a blow, the
creature ran off. His horse collapsed onto the
snow. As Ivan comforted the dying animal,
he realized that he was being watched.

"I'm sorry," said a rasping voice.

"I was so hungry... but I will make it up to you."

"How can you do that?" said Ivan bitterly. "How will I ever find the Firebird now?"

"Trust me," said the silver wolf. "Climb on my back, and I will take you to her."

Warily, Ivan climbed on. What else could he do?
Then, to his amazement, the wolf leaped into the
air. They soared over forests and hills until they
saw the distant lights of a palace.

"The Firebird is in the highest
room of the tallest tower," said
Silver Wolf. "Go and take
her, but be careful not to
touch her cage."

Ivan climbed the tower steps and found the Firebird, lighting up the whole room.

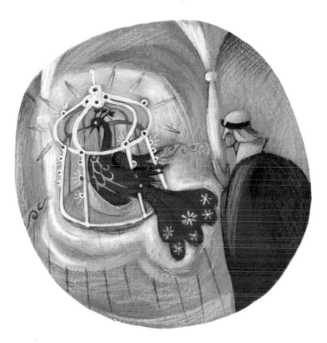

"How can I carry her without burning myself?" he wondered. "It can't be helped. I'll have to bring her cage."

Bells rang through the palace, guards stormed up the stairs and Ivan was thrown into the dungeons.

In the morning, he was brought before the king of the land, who looked at him curiously. "A prince, stealing my treasures in the night?"

Ivan told his story, and the king considered. "Well, perhaps we can make a bargain. You shall have the Firebird, if in exchange you will bring me the winged Horse of Power."

Silver Wolf knew just where to go. The pair flew on again, landing in the grounds of another palace.

"Listen," said Silver Wolf, "next to the horse you will see a bridle, set with jewels. Do not touch it."

Ivan soon found the Horse of Power in the stables. He reached for a plain halter, but his sleeve brushed the precious bridle. Shouts of alarm sounded through the palace.

Once again, Ivan spent a night in the dungeons before being taken to the king.

The king hardly noticed him. "What do horses matter?" he wept. "My daughter has been stolen!"

"She has been taken by the wicked wizard, Koshchey," Silver Wolf told Ivan, when at last he was freed. "You'll need all the luck you can get if you mean to rescue her. Many brave men have challenged Koshchey. He has defeated them all."

That evening, they soared over the high, craggy mountains to Koshchey's grim fortress.

Silver Wolf and Ivan landed in a garden
full of roses and statues: marble statues
of knights, with their swords raised.
With a shiver, Ivan realized what the
statues must once have been.
Beyond the statues, twelve beautiful
girls were dancing around a fountain.

Ivan only had eyes for the princess
watching them. Her smile was as bright
as the morning sun.

"Come quickly!" he called. "Silver
Wolf and I are here to bring you home!"

At that moment, there was a thunderclap and the castle door burst open. A towering figure strode out, surrounded by squealing demons.

"HOW DARE YOU?" roared Koshchey. "I am Koshchey the Deathless! I can never be defeated!"

"I have hidden my soul outside my body. This is my place of power, and I will turn you to stone." He raised his arms and began to cast his spell.

"His soul! It's in a box in the old tree stump," hissed Silver Wolf. It was too late. A terrible numbness was seeping through Ivan's body.

Then the wind whipped at his cloak and the Firebird's feather fluttered to his feet. Life and warmth surged through him once more.

Silver Wolf leaped at Koshchey, while Ivan scrabbled for the box. He opened it to reveal a gleaming golden egg.

With a howl, Koshchey saw what Ivan had found. "Stop!" he shrieked. "Stop and I'll give you anything you want!"

Ivan ignored him, hurling the egg to the ground where it smashed into pieces. There was a deafening roar, and the castle came crashing down.

When Ivan dared to look up, the sorcerer, his demons and all trace of his fortress were gone.

Ivan and Silver Wolf brought the princess safely home. When the old king saw his daughter again, he was overjoyed.

"The Horse of Power is not reward enough," he said, "and I can see how you feel about each other."

So Ivan and the princess were married, and the homecoming feast became a wedding banquet.

"Your father will want to see you," the king told
Ivan. "But may I travel with you some of the way?
I cannot say farewell to my daughter so soon."
And so they all flew to the Firebird's palace,
where the king stayed with the Horse of Power,
while Ivan and his bride
went on.

When Ivan's father saw them, his eyes filled
with tears. "My son! I thought you were lost."

"How could I have put you at risk? And as for
the Firebird... She should never be kept in a cage.
Let her come and go as she pleases, and eat apples
from my orchard whenever she likes."

From that day on, the Firebird was often seen darting among the jewel trees.

Sometimes she would let fall a golden apple, and another tree would grow from it. In time, that tree would bear fruit: not golden fruit, but still the sweetest apples in all the kingdom.

THE SORCERER'S APPRENTICE

Max had spent hours cleaning the sorcerer's workshop – and he still hadn't finished.

"I'm fed up," he moaned to Tabitha, the sorcerer's toad. "All I do is mop, scrub and polish. How will I ever learn any magic?"

"Max!" called a voice.

Max leaped from his chair as the sorcerer came into the workshop.

"I wondered if... Ugh!" The sorcerer lifted his foot in disgust. "Look at this toadstool. What *have* you been doing all morning?"

"Cleaning,"
Max said sulkily.
"Look, the water
tank is empty."

"You'd better
fill it up then,"
said the sorcerer.
"And sweep and scrub this floor again too.
You did a terrible job the first time."

Max sighed.

"I have to go into town," the sorcerer
went on, producing a shopping list.
"Hmm... must remember
dragons' scales. Now, don't
try any spells while I'm
out," he warned, "or I'll
turn you into a tadpole!"

With a glare at Max, he raised his arms. There was a flash of light. Purple smoke swirled around the room, and the sorcerer vanished.

"Hurray!" Max grinned. "A few hours off. I think I'll go for a swim in the moat."

"What about filling the water tank and scrubbing the floor?" Tabitha reminded him.

"The sorcerer won't be back for ages," said Max. "I'll do it later."

"He won't be happy..." said Tabitha.

"All right, all right," snapped Max, grabbing a broom and starting to sweep the floor. He groaned.

Filling the water tank would take ages, and lugging the pail up and down the steps from the pump to the tank was such hard work.

If only there were something he could do to speed things up...

And then he had a brilliant idea. A few days ago, the sorcerer had cast a spell on a broomstick and brought it to life.

"I just need to remember the spell," thought Max, "and then the broomstick can fill the tank for me!"

Max closed his eyes, took a breath and recited the magic words:

Root and branch of old oak tree

Bring this broom to life for me!

The broom shuddered in his hand...
and sprouted arms and legs.
"Fill up the water tank for me,"
ordered Max – and the broom did!

Max was delighted. His first ever spell had worked. "I'm worn out now," he yawned. "I think I deserve a little nap." And he stretched out on a chair and went to sleep.

The next thing he knew, a frantic toad was jumping up and down on his lap.

"Wake up! Wake up!" Tabitha croaked. "The tank is overflowing and the broom won't stop."

"Huh?" mumbled Max sleepily.

"Look!" said Tabitha.

"Oh no!" cried Max. The water had reached the top of the tank and was pouring over the side.

"That's enough!" Max told the broom. "You can stop now. STOP!"

The broom took no notice.

Back and forth it trotted, filling pails to the brim and pouring them into the water tank. Water sloshed in and sloshed straight out again, flooding onto the floor.

"PLEASE stop!" implored Max, but the broom kept going.

I can't look!

"Quick! Say a spell
to make it stop before it
floods the whole workshop," Tabitha pleaded.

"Um, I don't know another spell," said Max,
looking embarrassed.

"Of all the nincompoops..." muttered Tabitha.

By now, the water was up to his ankles, and still
the broom was bringing more.

"The sorcerer is going to be furious," Tabitha said. "There must be something you can do."

"I can't think of anything!" wailed Max.

"Could you chop it up?" suggested Tabitha.

"Great idea!" said Max.

With a loud CRACK! the broomstick split clean in two.

"Phew!" said Max, with relief.

And then he realized that each half of the broom was growing a new arm and leg.

"Two of them!" screamed Max. "What are we going to do now? Don't get any more water," he shouted at the brooms. "I don't need it. Do you hear me? NO MORE WATER!"

The brooms ignored him. Grabbing empty pails, they clattered up the steps to the pump, filled the pails and then rushed back down to the tank.

"I'm going to be in such trouble when the sorcerer comes back," Max thought gloomily.

"Please, please stop?" he tried one last time, but the brooms kept going, and they seemed to be speeding up.

Max sploshed through the water and tried
to grab them, but they darted out of his reach. By
now, the water was over his knees and rising fast...
past the top of his legs... creeping up to his waist...

Desperately, Max caught hold of a table as it
floated past.

The entire workshop was afloat and still the brooms kept filling the tank.

With a splash and a splosh, waves washed across the workshop.

"Help!" shouted Max. "Someone please help!"

"He warned you not to try any spells," Tabitha said. "Maybe next time you'll listen."

"You're not helping," said Max.

"Can anyone hear me? Please help us!" he yelled.

There was a loud POP! and the sorcerer appeared,
green stars glittering around him.

He looked down in horror as water lapped
at his robe.

What's going on?

"I leave you for just a couple of hours,"
he began, "and I return to find my workshop
is a swimming pool. What on earth have you
been doing?"

Just at that moment, the two brooms ran
down the stairs and flung yet more water
into the workshop.

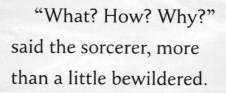

"What? How? Why?"
said the sorcerer, more
than a little bewildered.

"I thought I said no spells!" he spluttered.

Quickly, he spread his arms wide, held his wand high, and called out:

Eye of bat and tooth of boar,

Return to how you were before!

In a swirl of smoke one of the brooms vanished. The sorcerer waved a hand and the other broom swished across the floor, leaving a trail of stars. It came to rest against a table and leaned there, perfectly still.

With a glug-glug-glug, the water started to drain away, leaving battered books and an upturned cauldron behind.

Max peered over the edge of the water tank.

"I warned you, no spells!" snapped the sorcerer, raising his wand.

"I'm really, really sorry," Max gabbled. "*Please* don't turn me into a tadpole. I promise I won't meddle with magic again."

"Not good enough," said the sorcerer.

"That was quite a tricky spell he did," Tabitha pointed out. "Perhaps you should start teaching him magic? He is your apprentice after all."

The sorcerer thought for a moment.

"Hmm, maybe..." he grunted. "But first he can clean up in here. Without magic. And if you ever disobey me again," he added to Max, "you'll be frogspawn in the moat."

From that day on, Max was the ideal apprentice. He studied hard, and soon he had learned how to start spells *and* how to stop them.

When he grew up, he became a great sorcerer whose spells always worked perfectly – though he was careful never to enchant another broomstick.

PINOCCHIO

This is the story of Pinocchio the puppet. It begins with a piece of wood, propped up in a carpenter's workshop. The carpenter's name was Gepetto and he had decided to make a puppet.

"I'll call him Pinocchio," murmured Gepetto, as he carved a small, snub nose. "He'll be the son I never had."

Just then, the nose began to grow.

"How odd," thought Gepetto, trimming the wooden nose. He carefully carved a little mouth... and a red tongue poked out.

No sooner had Gepetto finished his puppet than it jumped to its feet. Snatching the carpenter's wig, it ran off down the lane.

"Oh no you don't!" shouted Gepetto, waving his chisel and racing after the puppet.

"Put that weapon down now,"
boomed a gruff policeman.
"Otherwise I'll arrest you for
threatening a puppet."

"Officer," Gepetto pleaded,
"that puppet is my son."

"And I'm the tooth fairy,"
chortled the policeman.

While Gepetto argued
with the policeman,
Pinocchio skipped back home.
He settled into Gepetto's chair
and warmed his feet by the fire.
"This is the life," he murmured.
"You foolish, selfish puppet,"
buzzed a voice.

Pinocchio looked up and saw a little cricket.

"You should be ashamed of yourself," the cricket said, "running away from your poor father!"

"Buzz off, you silly insect," piped Pinocchio.

The cricket gave a sigh. "Don't you want to be a *real* boy? Only good sons get the chance to become real."

"Leave me alone!" Pinocchio cried, and he threw a hammer at the cricket. THUD.

By now, the puppet was starving. He cracked open an egg to fry it, but out flew a chick.

"Bother!" huffed Pinocchio. "Where's Gepetto when you need him?"

Just then, the front door opened.

"Pinocchio?" called Gepetto. "You're safe!"

"And hungry," added Pinocchio.

Gepetto laughed and found
the puppet some food.

"I'll try to be good from
now on," said Pinocchio.

"Well, let's start by sending you to school," said Gepetto. He bought Pinocchio some clothes and a book, and sent him off to school.

"Come straight back after lessons!" he told him.

Pinocchio really did intend to go to school...
until he spotted a long line of people.

"What's going on?" he asked.

"We're waiting for the puppet show," answered
a friendly-looking man.

"Puppets!" said Pinocchio, and joined the line.

He had forgotten all about being
good. The second the doors
opened, he raced inside
to find the best seat.

Two famous puppets, Harlequin and Punchinello, pranced onto the stage. Their dances and tricks had the audience howling with laughter.

Halfway through they stopped, bent down and peered at Pinocchio. "Another puppet!" they cried. "Come and join us."

Before Pinocchio could say no, he was pulled on
stage and surrounded by excited puppets. They
bombarded him with questions and quite forgot
about the audience.

Soon there were boos from the crowd, followed
by a dreadful hush as a fierce man stormed up.

He whisked the puppets backstage
and glowered at Pinocchio. "You
ruined my show!" he growled.
"Sorry," said Pinocchio. "I was,
um, looking for my dad."
"Just get out of here,"
snarled the man. "Or
you'll be firewood."

Pinocchio didn't need telling twice. He raced off down the street, his nose itching as he ran. He could feel it growing longer and longer.

"Foolish, fibbing puppet," buzzed a familiar voice.

"Not you again," puffed Pinocchio.

He flicked the
cricket away, but
it was tricky to run
with a very long nose.
Pinocchio slumped down on
a patch of grass.

"I wish I'd gone to school," he said.
Instantly, his nose began to shorten. "I must
try harder to be a good son," he went on, and
his nose shrank back to its normal size.

"Cooooo!" called a pigeon. "Gepettooooo is
loooooking for yooooou."

"Where is he?" asked Pinocchio, quickly.

"I will take yooooou," the pigeon
replied. "Climb ontooooo my back."

The pigeon swooped the puppet into the sky and
they flew towards the coast. Far below, Pinocchio
saw a small boat setting out to sea.

He could just make out a silver-haired man
pulling at the oars.

"Dad?" cried Pinocchio.

At that very moment, a large wave engulfed the boat and it disappeared from view.

"Don't worry, I'll save you!" shouted the brave puppet. He leaped from the pigeon and dived into the ocean.

Pinocchio swam and swam until he could swim no more.

He was washed up, wet and miserable, onto a sandy beach. There was distant laughter, but poor Pinocchio was too exhausted to move.

Soon there were voices too.

"A puppet with no strings, imagine that."

"Is he asleep?"

"Maybe he's doing a seal impression."

"Who are you?" mumbled Pinocchio, opening his eyes. "Where am I?"

"Welcome to the Land of Lost Toys," said a lively jack-in-the-box. "Here, we only have fun, fun and more fun."

"Not me," said Pinocchio. "I'm too upset."

"Too upset to have fun?" scoffed a clown. "We'll see about that."

The toys lifted Pinocchio to his feet and gave him a tour of their island. It was one enormous funfair. In no time, Pinocchio was whooping with glee on the world's biggest roller-coaster.

"Are you a lost toy too?" asked a teddy bear.

"Er, yes," lied Pinocchio. His nose began to itch.

"The toys are my only family," said a rabbit.

"Me too," lied Pinocchio. His itchy nose began to grow longer.

"You foolish, fibbing puppet," buzzed a voice inside Pinocchio's head.

"Wait!" cried Pinocchio, suddenly thinking of Gepetto, adrift in his boat. "What am I doing? I must help my dad."

He clambered off the roller-coaster, sped down to the beach and waded into the water.

"I'm coming, Dad!" he yelled, as he swam out to sea. Then he felt a rush of water and everything went dark.

Pinocchio found himself in a squelchy tunnel. He saw a dim light in the distance and walked towards it, then stopped in amazement. There, sitting at a wooden desk, was a silver-haired man.

"Pinocchio?" whispered the old man.

"Dad!" the puppet exclaimed. "I promise I'll be good from now on. And I'll start by getting us out of here."

Pinocchio guided Gepetto along the dark, squelchy tunnel. They reached the mouth of a cave that was barred with pointy rocks. Across the moonlit sea, Pinocchio glimpsed dry land.

"We're going to swim for shore," he told his dad. "Don't be afraid. I'll help you."

Two drenched but happy figures arrived at
Gepetto's house late that night. The old man lit an
oil lamp and gazed in wonder at Pinocchio.

"Son!" he cried. "Just look at you. You're not a
puppet any more... You're a real boy!"

ABOUT THE STORIES

THE KING'S PUDDING

A folk tale from Indonesia. Mouse Deer is a popular character in Indonesian tales, always outwitting his enemies.

THE TIN SOLDIER

A story by Hans Christian Andersen. The original story had a very sad ending: the tin soldier fell into a fireplace and melted. All that was left of him was a heart-shaped piece of tin.

BEAUTY AND THE BEAST

This fairy tale was first written down by a French woman, Gabrielle de Villeneuve, in 1740. The version in this collection is based on Villeneuve's story and a retelling from 1756 by another French writer, Marie Le Prince de Beaumont.

WHY THE SEA IS SALTY

A folk tale from Korea. A similar story is told in Sweden.

THE STORY OF PEGASUS

This is a myth from Ancient Greece. Legend says that Pegasus sprang from the neck of a monster named Medusa, after her head was cut off.

DICK WHITTINGTON

This story is based on the life of a real person, Richard Whittington, who lived from about 1350 to 1423. He went to London to find work, became a successful cloth merchant and was mayor of London three times.

THE MAGIC GIFTS

A folk tale from Korea, originally titled 'The Three Gifts'.

THE FIREBIRD

A folk tale from Russia. One version of the story inspired a ballet with music by Igor Stravinsky.

THE SORCERER'S APPRENTICE

A tale that has been around for almost 2,000 years. The story retold here is based on a poem composed in 1797 by the German writer, Johann Wolfgang von Goethe.

PINOCCHIO

A story by Carlo Collodi, an Italian writer, whose real name was Carlo Lorenzini. Collodi was the name of the village where he was born.

Edited by Lesley Sims

Cover and additional illustrations: Lorena Alvarez

Digital imaging: Nick Wakeford & John Russell